MARGARET

A ZOMBIE APOCALYPSE HORROR STORY

WHEREVER HELENA GOES, THE LAMBS ARE SURE TO DIE.

MARIE F CROW

Copyright

Table of Contents

Copyright 3

Table of Contents 5

Chapter 1 10

Chapter 2 15

Chapter 3 18

Chapter 4 25

Chapter 5 29

Chapter 6 33

Chapter 7 39

Chapter 8 43

Chapter 9 48

Chapter 10 50

Chapter 11 54

Chapter 12 57

Chapter 13 60

Chapter 14 63

Chapter 15 67

Chapter 16 69

About the Author 71

About the Publisher 73

Sharp, crisp clicking of a woman's heels echoes off the walls like a ricocheting gunshot. It vibrates the walls, leaving an aftermath of panic with its sounds. Those caught in her path scatter with the sound that is aiming towards them like a warning. A warning that there is something very wrong today and it is only growing worse.

She inspires no cheerful greetings to start the day as she passes the other scientists unfortunate enough to find themselves near her. Emotionless eyes are locked ahead of her steps, refusing to acknowledge how she is being perceived. Her lab coat billows around her small frame lending an extra emphasis to her desperation to reach her destination. It is not the cape of a hero that she is wearing today like she had planned, but the cloak of a reaper that floats behind her, filling the space between her and those she passes.

"Have you heard?" The male's voice belongs to one of the few that match her prestige in this building. His steps falter, trying to keep up with her pace and his voice is not the icy shards with which hers radiates.

"Not here." She chills him with her rebuttal. It is the first time her eyes have removed themselves from the direction marked as forward in her path and they gaze now at the many faces pretending to not watch them pass. The very thing she was hoping to avoid fills the hushed tones of the hall. Panic.

With a glare that would cause Hell itself to cringe, she stares at the man beside her, slides her plastic encrypted card through the security process and enters a room where there has not been silence in days. Anger and blame has scarred this room and those inside it. All communication is now a blend of pointed fingers and raised voices with the attempt to pass the fault of the fallout on another. Truth is, the fault belongs with each one of them. Their raised voices and argumentative words will not spare them from this truth.

"If you would…?" Her voice leaves no room for the question; it seems to form and there are none that risk asking.

Voices lower as those in the room collect their emotions. Chairs slide against the short, woven carpet as the room comes to order. The Ice Queen is taking her throne and she may very well be the only one left with the courage to command them.

"As you all are aware, the vaccine has had unexpected results. With no resources left to combat those results, we must now focus our efforts on containment. We have already begun reaching out to all those who are scheduled to receive the vaccine today and prepared them for any potential side effects." Her voice held the emotions of the room at bay. It did, until she spoke the last words.

The room becomes anger tainted again with the repetition of the words "side effects." It is said with many accents, many tones and with many emotions, but it is always said with anger.

"Yes, side effects. At this time, we are unable to justify any other explanation for what has occurred. Tests are still being run on the current subjects we hold. We feel confident we will isolate this new mutation and eradicate it, making the vaccine viable again. This is just a minor set-back."

The room explodes again with emotions and insults.

"How many shipments have been released?" A woman with soft blonde hair and genuine concern shouts over the male disputes.

"All of them." The Ice Queen hates having to answer that question, knowing the reactions it will cause, and it does.

"All of them being...?" Is a joined chorus of many pitches from in front of her.

"Every ordered shipment to the schools, government, and medical facilities." She fights to keep her face under control. This day was supposed to be the highlight of her career, marking her as a genius to not only her colleagues but to the world. Today, they will mark her for life, but not as anything she will want to carry on her transcript.

"Right now we are sending out every available trained personnel we have to help combat the side effects in the larger areas." No one will remember how hard she has tried to counter the inevitable. They will only remember her for the destruction.

"Is there anything else we can do?" The room finally grows to true silence.

"Go home. Hug your families. Tell your friends how much you love them. Wait. All we can do now, is wait." Her voice finally holds an emotion and it seals the room in dread.

How does one wait for the end of mankind, as the world knows it, to arrive? What preparations do you take to secure yourself in a world where the day holds only questions? How do you explain to your family the sudden need for seclusion without scaring them, or alerting anyone else, causing panic?

What moral compass now points true north when you hold the knowledge of what is about to happen to those around you? Do you pray for forgiveness or for salvation? Do you bother to pray at all?

Chapter 1

I don't want to go to school today. Today is the day of the school-wide vaccines that have been ordered to help fight against the many winter ailments that can spread like wildfire through a school this time of the year. We will be brought into the nurse's office one by one to receive the shot with no amount of pleading or crying to save us from her, or her needle of doom. Tears will only result in many mocking jokes made about us for the rest of the year, if not longer. Already the horror stories are circulating about the pain the shot will bring, and the size of the needle that will be used. Obviously, I don't want to go to school today.

I can hear the birds singing. I can see the sun peeking through the blinds on my windows, making odd little shapes on the cream-colored carpet of my bedroom. They are telling me it is time to wake up with their subtle hints, but I don't want to.

I can smell the thick scent of breakfast in the air of my room. It makes my stomach rumble with its craving of the warm bacon that my father calls "pig flesh". I try not to think of it like that. Nothing with the term flesh in it sounds like something I want to eat. The heavy scent of pancakes and sweet syrup weigh the air down with the depressing fact that morning is here, but I don't want to get up, yet.

Soon, my mother will be here to wake me. She will sing her normal, "Good Morning" song with her perky voice, as she has always done every morning that I can remember, while she lays out my clothes to wear. It is inevitable that I will eventually be forced out of my warm bed and have to start my day. All of this will lead up to my going to school. I don't want to go to school today.

I hear my door slide across the thick carpet and I squeeze my eyes tight. I hope she will leave me alone for just a little longer if she thinks that I am still soundly sleeping. I know she won't, but I hope so just the same.

"Good morning. Good morning. I sing hello to you. Good morning. Good morning. Won't you sing hello, too?" My mom sings her normal song, and I know all my hopes are wasted. I cringe, not from her voice, well not completely from her voice, but mostly from the inability to escape any longer from her.

"Time to get up sleepy head." My father sits on the foot of my bed with the attempt to   double team me today. I still have a Plan B though.

Holding onto my throat, I roll over onto my back and cough. Exaggerating my face with the make-believe pain of swallowing, I look to him and try to force sadness into my eyes.

"I don't feel good. I think I am already sick. So, I don't need to go today anyway. It is probably best if I just stay home."

My father chuckles at me while patting my feet that are hiding under the blankets. "No such luck, Margaret." He leans over me, kissing my forehead. His tie dangles between us with its crisp pattern of slanted lines and I know he will be leaving for work soon. That will leave me only with Mother to have to convince to keep me home. Sometimes my,   "sad eyes" work better on her anyway.

"No fever," he tells me, with a wink to my mom. "I think the only sickness you have is a classic case of nerves. Lucky for you, your mom has the perfect antidote waiting downstairs. A hot breakfast and well packed lunch. Now let's move, Scooter, before it grows cold."

"If it is cold, it is obviously not the perfect antidote and I will just stay sick. I better just not risk it and stay in bed." I cough again and roll to my side, half out of the feeling of desperation and the other half trying to hide my disappointment that Plan B is not going as well as I had planned for it to.

"If it is cold it is your own fault and you will just have to enjoy it that way." His voice holds that warning tone that Dads sometimes have, and I know that it is not working on him.

He pulls the covers from me, making my body shiver with the sudden temperature change. Fall is here, but some mornings it feels as if it is already slowly fading into winter allowing the house to be chilly in the mornings. It only adds to my already growing reluctance to leave my bed.

Most days I do not mind the morning routine of getting ready for school. Most days I like school. I enjoy Art class the most. The chipper Mrs. Schulz makes the class enjoyable with her warm smile and mischievous eyes, but it is the painting that I enjoy the most. The swirling of many various colors together to make deeper colors, or new colors altogether, to paint with is like exploring new lands for me. With these new colors, I can paint the grass of my pictures or the skies of them whatever color I want. It is a new land of my creation and I love it.

On the weekends, I often wake my parents with the sounds of my cartoons and my attempts of pouring the milk into my bowl of cereal. Some days, most of the milk makes it into the bowl even. Some days, I do not wake them at all and I can enjoy eating in the living room rather than at the kitchen table. It makes watching my cartoons seem like a hidden secret when I do that. I love that, too.

Today, I do not want to get up. There is not a thing I love about today so far. I do not want to go through the routine that will force me to be at school. Something bad is happening at school today. Something that I, and so many of my friends, do not want to do.

My father gives me a playful pat, signaling that he is over my attempts of refusing to accept the fact that I am going to school today. I sigh dramatically, voicing my opinion under the radar, at what they are making me do. They are still not moved by my unwillingness, though. My mother turns to my closet, with her silent refusal to save me from my father, to pick an outfit that will somehow make all of this better. Unless, she has stashed a pony in my closet while I was sleeping, nothing is going to make today better, but she is still going to try.

"How about a pretty dress today?" I am not sure if she is talking to herself or me. If it is to me, then the answer is "no".

Lilly Hawthorn always has better dresses anyway. The thought fills me with bitterness for my classmate. A Teacher's Pet title does not even really begin to embrace her perfection.

"Can I wear my blue one? With the flowers? With the jacket?" It is my favorite combination. It makes me feel pretty. Not as pretty as Lilly, but still pretty.

"Sure, Scooter," she tells me, pulling the ensemble out of my closet that she keeps so well organized. "Do you want your boots or tennis shoes?"

"Tennis shoes. The boots hurt my toes last time." I wiggle my toes, remembering how the boots pinched them together.

"Well, we can't have hurt toes." She reaches for my still wiggling toes, trying to tickle them, but I am too fast for her. I tuck my feet up under me and laugh at her attempt.

Maybe it won't be so horrible today after all. It is just a shot, right? A perky voice whispers in my head. I'm not sure who it belongs to yet, but I know it is not completely mine. I have no perk in my 'tude.

"Get dressed and then come downstairs to eat. After that, we will brush our teeth and fix our hair. How will you wear yours today?" She always says we but it is never, "we."

My mother is already dressed and her hair, that matches the red shade of my own, is already pulled back into a high ponytail. I think she just likes to feel included.

"Pig tails with white ribbons!" I answer triumphantly. Lilly's hair is too fine to stay in pigtails all day but mine isn't. My mother has a secret weapon for frustrating frizz and escaping strands. She calls it hairspray. She uses a lot of hairspray.

I watch my parents leave my room together, holding hands. My father smiles at me, giving me a wink to encourage my good behavior. I want to make them happy, but my stomach is rumbling with something different now and it does not fill me with encouragement.

I am afraid of what Charlotte said about today. She told us that the shots are huge needles because of all the things it is supposed to help fight against. Our whole arm will go limp and then it will bruise, making it painful to move. We won't be able to play on the swings or jump rope at recess. There will be no games of tag or hide-and-seek. Just the many sore arms and our pouting, sad faces.

If they give it in the wrong arm, we may not even be able to move it to eat lunch. They will then have to give it in the other arm to fix the mistake! It only works if it is placed in the right arm, she said, and I am not sure if she meant the right arm or the "right arm". How are we supposed to know? Will they know? If we cry, we will get two shots in the same arm if it is wrong or not and I always cry. I guess that means I will not be eating the special lunch my mom packed for me today. I bet it has a cupcake.

Charlotte's dad is a lawyer and he has told her all of this. She said he is super smart because he has all of these special things he has to do for his job everyday, so he must be right. She said so and no one argues with Charlotte. It doesn't end well if you argue with Charlotte. It's way worse than getting shots.

I give my stuffed lamb one final tight hug before leaving my warm bed. His fluffy body always comforts me when I am scared, but today it doesn't have the normal feeling. The stitched smile he wears doesn't seem as happy today. Nor do his black button eyes seem as bright. His white body is a hue of a darker shade of white, as if he is covered in dust, but I still wish I could find a way to sneak him into my book bag even with his strange change in attitude. We both might feel braver if he was with me, even if it is our secret. We are not allowed to take stuffed animals to school though and I don't want to get into trouble today. They might give me three shots, in the wrong arm even!

Chapter 2

I am waiting for my goodbye hug from my father at the front door with his heavy, brown briefcase in my hands. I like the rich smell of its leather. The leather collects the saturating smells of his day and they each remind me of him. It is a swirl of his morning coffee and of his very male cologne adding to the incense of the cigars he sneaks at work, thinking that Mom doesn't know. She does. Mom knows a lot of things we don't want her to know. She just doesn't always tell us that she knows until she needs to tell us. If she needs to tell us, that normally means we are in trouble. I like to let her keep her secrets. It is better for all of us that way.

He is already on the phone, setting up his appointments for today and I have to wait silently for my good-bye hug. He is moving meetings around and scheduling his lunch while I stare at his shoes. They shine, reflecting the light of the room with the amount of attention he spends on them every night.

I know that inside this leather bag, his files are stored in colored paper binders with the alphabetical order of his clients written neatly on inserted tabs. I know because he sits for an hour every night sorting the piles, labeling them with the correct names, and then he will pull out the dark shades of the polish for his shoes. This is, "Daddy's Hour." The hour that

I must entertain myself, not make a lot of noise, or run around the house. It is a long hour, trust me.

His jacket matches the dark shade of his slacks. His shirt and tie contain the only colors he has chosen to wear today. Even his sunglasses, that cling with one arm in the pocket of his slacks, are dark rimmed. It reminds me of an uncle's funeral with so many half-interested conversations and dark-clothed people. I had to sit silently through that, too.

He winks at me, noticing me waiting for him for the first time. He takes the heavy briefcase that has begun to feel like a suitcase while I have waited patiently for my hug. He ruffles my red curls, that he believes my mom and I gain our tempers from, before heading out the door. He is still talking to whomever is on the other side of that conversation and never looks back at me when he closes the car door.

I watch my father's black sedan retreat silently from the driveway through the large window and I know with a heart crushing truth that I am not going to be getting my good-bye hug today. He forgot me.

"Scooter?" my mother is calling to me, but I stand still, frozen, watching the black car as it makes its way down the street with high hopes that he will turn around. He will return with a big smile and an apology covered in tight hugs and kisses to make up for it. When I watch the last view of it turn the corner, I know I am watching in vain. I sigh and make my way to the kitchen where Mom is waiting. I would have really liked a good-bye hug today.

My plate is waiting for me at the high kitchen island. The dark granite of the counter mirrors my mood after being so easily forgotten by the man I look to for protection and guidance. She has made a smiley face out of the pancakes, bacon, and eggs. The bacon smiles as proudly as she does at me with my discovery. She knows that he forgot my hug and is trying to make up for it. Moms do that. Sometimes, Moms have to do that a lot.

I start my breakfast with the fluffy yellow hair fashioned from the eggs because I hate them the most. They are spongy and moist, feeling weird on my tongue. They slide down my throat with cold lumps like oatmeal left out too long. I will save the bacon for last. It's better when it is crunchy from sitting, anyway. So, it will sit and it will wait just as I did moments ago, but unlike Dad, I won't forget.

Who could forget bacon? I ask myself. *My Dad. I bet my Dad could.*

I watch my Mom dance around the kitchen cleaning up the many pans used to cook breakfast. She sings off key with her songs filling the breakfast fragrant kitchen. She sings into whichever cooking utensil she has in her hand at the time of high notes like a make believe radio Diva. Her long ponytail swings back and forth with her movements. Her brown boots click on the tiles, keeping beat with the music from the radio as she cleans. Her smile is contagious and my sour mood can't win against it. I smile at her between bites of my breakfast. Her antics are helping me to forget about the missing hug and the disappointment it causes me. Moms do that.

They keep secrets. They make special breakfasts and pack special lunches. They help with your hair; tying perfect bows with the ribbons no matter how many attempts it takes, or the words muttered under breaths. They dance around knowing how silly they look just for a smile. And they never, ever, forget good-bye hugs.

Chapter 3

My hair is held high in pretty white ribbons that refused to tie evenly at first, resulting in Mom whispering words that I thought only Dad knew. The perfectly arched bows are securing two perfect red pigtails that spiral down around my face with many layers of hairspray holding them firm and thicker than the paste that our teacher calls glue. I can feel them patting my cheeks when I turn my head and I smile with the sensation. The spirals bounce as I tilt my head from side to side with the music in my mom's car. She is still attempting to sing along with the songs that surround us with their upbeat rhythms. There is no shot of a singing television show try-out in her future, but I love her voice just the same.

The car line wraps around the school with the extra amount of nervousness of today's well known event. Kids that would normally ride the bus are being driven in today with the extra hugs and kisses needed to encourage them through the morning. An excess of teachers have been brought out in their bright orange vests to help direct the traffic, and dislodge stubborn kids from their parent's arms or legs with gentle smiles to mask their annoyance. My mother sings extra loud as we watch the added confusion and I feel as if I am being hauled off to something much worse than a school day with her over emphasis of false cheer.

"Good morning, Margaret! Are you ready for school today?" Mrs. Schinder asks me, as she opens my door. It is a shock to see her out from behind her long desk in the main office. A shock that I know my face did not cover well.

Normally she holds the position of school secretary as formidable as a military commander holds his squad in check. To have her out among the teachers is a sure sign of the breakdown of control or the amount of extra concern that has been taken for today. It does not help to calm my rumbling stomach at all. Between her and my mother, I may be honestly sick.

"Scooter, it won't be so bad, ok?" my mother's voice is sof,t and holds the same comforting pitch used after a nightmare. "Your father and I are meeting for lunch and then we will be seeing the doctor to get ours, too. After dinner, we will all go out for ice cream. The three of us. We can swap stories over who cried the most, ok?" She smiles at me while twisting a section of my hair around her long delicate finger with genuine concern. My stomach is not convinced.

"I bet your dad will cry the most," she whispers it, with a hidden smile, and I join her in the enjoyment of the thought of my tall father sobbing like a baby in a white, sterilized doctor's office.

"That will teach him for forgetting me and not hugging me good-bye," I whisper back, almost ashamed of my enjoyment at the thought of him crying. Almost.

"You bet it will!" She wrinkles her nose while smiling at me before giving me a wink in female solidarity.

She kisses my forehead as Mrs. Schinder drums her fingers on the car door, growing impatient with our delay. "Don't let the troll bully you," she whispers one final good-bye, before I exit the car, as we are unable to prevent it any longer.

She keeps pace with me as she pulls forward through the long, winding line. We make faces at one another through the lowered window until she is forced with the flow of traffic to drive away. She waves one more time into the rear-view mirror at me and I fight my stomach to be brave.

I am not a baby like some kids that are still clinging to their parents, afraid of the shot and the possibilities of the stories they have been told. I am not on the outside, anyway. On the inside, I desperately want her car to turn around and come get me. Just like last time, I watch a car's tail lights before the red glow from her brakes slips from view. This car doesn't turn around either. It also keeps going straight ahead into the day, so, so do I.

Pulling my rolling, soft pastel colored book bag behind me, I walk to my normal morning group of friends in our normal morning spot. The wheels catch on the segments of the walkway, making a clumping noise when the wheels overcome the cement obstacles. It sounds like a beating heart. This false heart is beating with the same speed as my very real one. Both pound in my ears with each step that I am taking that leads me closer to the school's entrance.

It's just a shot, right? Has become my silent mantra of courage in my mind. If I repeat it enough, I may even start to believe it.

Charlotte stands in the middle of our group like every normal school morning. She is wearing her dark jeans and a billowing style of a shirt. Today, it is a bright neon color that helps her to stand out even more among us with the over dramatic flair that she enjoys. She is also taller than the rest of us. Now, draped in the bright color, she seems to tower over us. Her boots shine with their high quality brown leather that reaches higher on her legs than most would dare at our age. Her lips are a deeper hue than they should be with the lip-gloss she has placed upon them. Something, also, the rest of us would not dare to do.

My parents call her family "new money," I am not sure where one gets "new" money from, but Charlotte sure does like to show it off from the perfectly salon colored hair on her head to her high fashion book bag. All of it has to match and today is no exception. My dress doesn't seem as pretty as it did a few hours ago. I slide into the space between April and Teddy as Charlotte, once again, begins to spread horror stories of what is to come with great theatrical renditions of what she knows to be true.

"They will line us all up and then this giant machine will be aimed at our arms. When we stand next to it, it will shoot this huge needle into our arm like those sliding doors in the stores that just sense when someone is near. This chemical will then swim through our body with all these viruses in it. But the viruses are, like, dead so we won't get sick from them." Charlotte uses impressive hand gestures to accent her impressive knowledge on a very impressive situation. One of us is not impressed.

"We are going to have dead stuff inside us?" April's face sours with the thought.

"I had a dead fish once. It didn't swim at all." Meghan shrugs, implying she doesn't believe Charlotte, but not willing to actually say it. Yet.

"Not, like, that kind of dead. Like, a different dead," Charlotte says this, as if it should make perfect sense now to us with her definite clarification of the matter. It doesn't. At least not to me.

"Dead is dead. How can something move if it is dead?" Meghan continues to push the boundaries of Charlotte's logic with her stubbornness to fall in line like the rest of us good soldiers.

"It's a different type of dead and you're just too stupid to understand it." Charlotte folds her arms across her chest, unhappy to have her words doubted. It is a very, "so there" posture.

"*I'm* not the one that believes dead things can move around. My dog didn't move. My fish didn't move. That's how you know something is dead. They *don't* move." Meghan stands firm with her voice and posture about her beliefs on the matter like a Christian on a Crusade.

Neither Charlotte's crossed arms nor her glare affects Meghan. She is the only one that it doesn't. The rest of us have already begun to take hidden steps backwards, afraid of the reaction Charlotte will have with the gauntlet thrown at her feet.

Whatever that explosion may have been, Meghan is saved from as the loud chime of the bell sends its normal three rings across the green grass of the yard. Charlotte's glare hints that this is not over yet. With teachers corralling the large amount of kids that mingle together at the entrance today, it is easy to slip away from those hate-filled eyes when we separate into our class groups, but we still keep our steps in a backwards retreat though. Just in case.

Charlotte is the oldest, requiring her to leave first. Her hair swings with her anger over not being able to defend her logic from what she views as an attack instead of a conversation. Who knows, maybe it was an attack. Meghan is not a huge fan of Charlotte to begin with. Everyone knows that and we were reminded of it.

I'm more concerned with the large machine that will be used to give us the shot than over what the shot is, or what it may do or not do to my body. The idea of dead things swimming around inside me does not make me feel any better though. Or, the not really dead things, depending on who you want to believe. Either way, my stomach does not approve.

April's face is still contorted with wrinkles of concern over it. "Do you think she meant like dead, dead? Or, just like …." her voice trails off, unsure of what else dead could be, but dead.

"Maybe it is one of those medical things that doesn't make sense unless you have a big framed piece of paper on a wall behind a big wooden desk," I offer, as the only hope I have to understand it all myself.

She nods, seeming to be content with my answer.

If only Charlotte was so easily convinced of such things. I roll my eyes with the thought. Santa will come in July before Charlotte would ever agree with another.

April, Teddy, and I walk along the brightly colored purple and teal halls leading to our classroom. Normally, we would skip along the patterned tiles, avoiding the, "cracks" as we call out the classic rhyme. Today though, we march, lifeless, along the brightly painted halls with each of us lost in our own mental debates over what today will bring for us.

Our silence presents our teachers with added concerns as they watch us file into the rooms with our silent foreboding. The whole school is more restrained today with the knowledge of what lies ahead. We pout and sulk, knowing we are unable to avoid it with the grace that only those of our youth can get away with and master.

We flop into desks. Book bags, "accidentally" fall too hard from shoulders, hitting the floor with loud, unnecessary noises. Arms cross, eyes glare and lips frown all in silent conversations. Conversations that express our moods and the thoughts that are transforming us into the cranky, moody creatures that now fill the room.

Our teacher's name is Mrs. Mary Lamb. Seriously, I can't make this stuff up. Of course, this means that our room is themed after the classic nursery rhyme. At the start of the school year, we were each asked to make our own cotton stretched lamb to place along the wall to display our names like dining table place mats marking our territories. Now, the room is filled with different designs of white lambs and their black drawn eyes of many sizes.

I named mine after my own lamb from home even if my name is written on the pink collar around its neck. This way, he truly is with me everywhere I go. His bright colored smile is not as comforting as the one that awaits for my return home, but it helps as he stares down at me from his high place on the wall to brighten long school days, like today.

The rest of the room's walls are painted in a vivid mural depicting rolling green hills of a countryside scene. It winds around the room to focus on Mrs. Lamb's desk, framing her within the classic story of a girl and her lamb's trip to school. I used to find it pleasant and peaceful. Now it seems too bright for a room filled with so many silent frowns.

Today's schedule is placed upon the board, but the only entry our eyes see is the one labeled, "special activity" and it falls far down on the list, making the day loom long and depressing before us. Nervous glances are passed around the room with each new set of eyes that finds the time slot. The shared horror stories of the potential possibilities of what may happen are easy to read among the many faces of my classmates. It brings forth new versions with each sigh as we all wonder what the other has heard and who has the truth.

If there was even a truth that was told? I wonder, with all the many stories that float around, and each of them being more horrible than the last.

Busy work is waiting on the desks to entertain the ones already here while the time passes for each student to make their way into the classroom. Normally, it is activities blurred with the current spelling list or main topic of a subject disguising it as an attempt at fun.

They are rarely ever fun. Today we have a coloring sheet that has nothing to do with any topics we have held for the past week, or year for that matter. It is a blatant attempt to distract our minds from the very thing they are soaking in. The fact that Mrs. Lamb is trying so hard to distract us from the "special activity" makes it seem that much larger of a threat. The busy work has failed.

The distraction only coaxes a select few into ease of mind. These are the same ones that we often find easily distracted with bright colors or shiny objects. Some stare in panic, trying to remember what the scene in front of them is supposed to link back to as if some important fact of the past lesson has slipped from them and now taunts them. Some have caught on, like myself, to the reason for such a detour from the typical and are glancing around to see if they are the only ones. We hold a silent conversation when we meet the gaze of another that recognizes the truth. For something that our parents told us would be so simple, there sure is a lot of, "to do" to avoid it from not only them, but now the school as well. If a pony were to walk in right now, I would know that I am doomed.

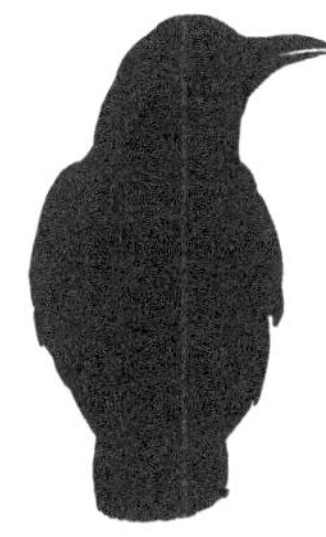

Chapter 4

"At this time," Mrs. Schinder's voice comes over the school's speakers, and we all stand, programmed to do so by the many mornings spent following the same routine. Today though, the routine is about to be thrown out and the confusion it causes stirs more than just trouble for the teachers. "We will have all staff, excluding teachers and office support, to report to the gym for their vaccinations."

Just the word finally said aloud by the school's personnel, results in many shuffling and hushed, whispering voices. The elephant in the room has finally been acknowledged and it frees us to speak of it. Some speak, some just start to cry. Someone find something shiny, stat!

"Teachers, please disregard all previous planning for the student vaccinations. At this time, please go ahead and start lining up your students and wait for further instructions."

The loud sound of the system being disengaged with its loud rattling is the only sound now that is echoing through the painted overly pastel halls. The combination of the words, "students" and "vaccinations" has stolen all speech from not only us, but the teachers as well.

Adults have a way of reading between the lines that we have not yet grasped. They no longer spell out words but punctuate the silence with hidden looks and expressions. Something about the sentence, other than the obvious inclinations, is twisting Mrs. Lamb's normally pretty face into many deep wrinkles of concern. She looks like she may need some busy work now, too.

Rows of eyes are resting on her as we wait for instructions. We are all still standing, waiting for the Pledge that never comes. There is no, "Star Spangled Banner" today. There is just a prolonged moment of silence in our confusion.

Mrs. Lamb rearranges the papers on her desk to mask her lack of knowledge that has prompted the schedule change, but she still instructs us just the same. A good teacher is not just one that can lead a class, but also one that can hold control under any circumstance. We learned the first week in the school year that Mrs. Lamb is not afraid of being in control.

"Let's go ahead and clean up our areas and pack away our book bags under our desks. Go ahead and leave that sheet on your desk. We will work on it later." Her face may still hold confusion, but there is no room for any in her demeanor.

The room becomes alive with sounds as coloring materials are stored in zipper pouches to be packed away. The zipper teeth mingle their sounds with worried whispers and the sliding of fabric along the tiles as bags are secured as instructed. Normally, this is where April and I would mimic an airplane flight attendant with the routine line of making sure all trays are in their upright position. There is no comedy to be inspired today though, but our eyes still meet out of habit.

Hers are no longer the soft pastel of teal coloring I am used to seeing. They are faded and dull with worry as the many tall tales are circulating in her mind. We thought we had time to prepare ourselves for this. We should have held the time span of many hours still before forming this line. There should have been time to disprove the rumors, building courage in our over-beating hearts that race as reality is upon us with questions asked to those that went before our time.

It is just a shot, right? A shot with many needles, from a machine that will force not really dead things into us, making our arms grow numb, unable to withstand the amount of pain that it will cause.

No big deal at all. My sarcasm has no bounds.

One by one, we make our way to the, "waiting wall." This is where we form the long line of our class before making our way to any place in the building. There is no need for any extra words of caution about behavior. We are somber already, standing silent like an army awaiting a battle to come. Perhaps we are closer to mourners awaiting the march out of the church. Either way, as the line reluctantly grows, we are ready to follow the procedure, even if we are not ready for the results.

Half of us grow anxious as the room grows dark with the lights being turned off in the final countdown of departure. The other half grows more somber, retreating into some private place of security to conceal their concerns. I bounce between each half as one moment I am lured into the fears and the next I take deep breaths to escape the panic.

"Maybe we will get cartoon Band Aids," I whisper to April.

My voice shocks her from her own thoughts and she startles a little from it before turning to me with those still lackluster eyes. "What?" her voice is paper-thin.

Normally, whispering in line is an art form perfected to avoid the ever watchful eyes of our teacher. Today, we don't hold the enthusiasm to play the game and are overly bold.

Perhaps being forced to the back of the line would not hold the normal threat today? I think about it, but the risk to my spotless record will not agree with me.

"Like in the doctor offices. You go in, and they have all these different Band Aids to choose from. I wonder if they will have any." The look April gives me makes me wonder what has grown on my face while I was talking. She peers at me as if I have just spoken a foreign language and she can either not understand me or believe me. My father gives me that look, a lot. You know, when he remembers me.

"Just trying to find something positive," I mutter, shrugging with the rejection.

"Do you think the dead things will live in us forever?" April is still holding onto the fears from earlier.

What will happen when she catches up to the needle rumors?

"She said they are not really dead, but even so, how can anything that is any level of dead live anywhere? Isn't that the whole point of being dead?" My answer only causes more questions.

It is starting to sound like one of those never ending debates on talk shows my father enjoys. The boringly dressed men sit around in overly large black chairs, "discussing" a current topic without any of them really holding any real answers to the questions. They just like to talk, my mother tells me whenever I ask what the point of the shows is. To think he prefers those to cartoons still baffles me.

Dancing bears, people, really. Who wouldn't love dancing bears? I will never understand the man.

"So, they will just be floating inside us forever?" There is no misunderstanding her opinion of that with her facial expression.

"I guess? I haven't thought much about it." It is the truth. I am still caught in the net of fears over the needle. My mind has not escaped past that yet.

"It's just so gross." April has no other comments to share as she slips back into her inner world of turmoil.

Where do dead things go? They are put in dark wooden coffins to be placed into deep rectangles of removed earth. Slowly, that earth is replaced, shovel by shovel, sob by sob, securing the dead forever inside. We then place monuments marking the spot to forever remember what we can no longer see. The needle is the coffin. Our bodies are the earth. The scar is the monument. But, we won't remember. Not until it is time to bury the dead again, anyway.

Chapter 5

The line moves slowly down the hallways that are refusing the mood of its occupants with its patterned pastel walls. The colors seem overly done with so many dismal steps

being placed on the colorful floor tiles. We are once again locked in a prolonged moment of silence, not out of respect for the rules, but for the fears that whisper into each ear with targeted effects.

Our line joins with other lines like a disjointed train as we make our way to the gym. Leaders become followers time and time again with the continued growth of the train, until due to the length, we are forced to wait along the wall for the double metal doors of the gym to open. They stand with their purple coloring, closed and blocking the sight of our doom that we are all anxiously awaiting.

The teachers whisper to one another as their eyes glide over their charges. There are shared words over and over with each new arrival of "not how we were told" and "anyone knows why the change." Their sentence structure may change each time, but it is always the same thought process. Basically, they all blame Mrs. Schinder. Just as my mother normally does, too.

The sounds of the metal doors opening pulls every head of those in the hallway towards it. It must be unnerving to be the focal point of so many eyes, and Mrs. Tawny and Mrs. Bell stumble from it. We try to peer past them into the hidden room to catch a peek at the hidden secrets within but it is impossible. The doors slide closed, keeping their private information away from us.

The cafeteria's staff stares at the sea of scared eyes and melts with the emotions encircling them. They still wear their morning coats with the change in timing not allowing them the time to place their personal items in their private areas. They try to comfort us as they pass with smiles and gentle touches, but the emotion never carries into those they reach.

"How bad did it hurt?" Teddy's voice echoes the thoughts circling in everyone's mind.

With a smile, Mrs. Tawny removes her coat and rolls up her work shirt to show us a brightly colored Band Aid. My eyes light up seeing the very thing I had hoped would at least be a small bonus from today.

"Told ya' so," I whisper to April, pointing at the suggested prize from earlier.

"It only burns a little and then it is over. I promise." Mrs. Tawny smiles at all the lingering doubts worn like well-fitted gloves on our faces.

"Just a bee sting and then done," Mrs. Bell offers, trying to support her friend's advice.

Why is it always bees? Does no other insect ever bite? Fire ants bite, but no one ever says "just a fire ant bite." It is always "just a bee sting." I wonder these thoughts as they roll around in my mind. *What did bees do so long ago to earn them such a bad rap in our eyes? Do the other insects ever get jealous?*

"Do you think we should tell them?" Mrs. Bell's eyes slide over to her coworker with a hidden, sly smile.

"They told us we shouldn't…" Mrs. Tawny's words hang in the air like a dare to the powers that be, or for caution to the fact they may be listening.

"I think they can keep a secret." Mrs. Bell whispers the word, "secret" emphasizing the need for discretion making it sound all the more enticing to us.

"I don't know. Can you keep a secret?" Mrs. Tawny turns to us with mischievous intentions.

The hallway erupts into a chorus of, "yes" and "uhuhs" with the idea of a secret being too much to contain the rules of the hallway anymore.

"Well ok, but remember, you can't tell anyone else." Mrs. Tawny is now enjoying the game as much as we are as the space fills with our loud agreements in many excited pitches.

With as much mystery that has been injected into the secret, she could tell us that we all have spelling words to write tonight, just as we do every night, and we would still all cheer. Well, for a small moment anyway.

"We were just on our way to start making a very special treat for you today. Mrs. Tawny and I have been storing it in our closet in the back of the kitchen just for today! Any guess as to what it might be?" With the ending of Mrs. Bell's question the hallway explodes with many guesses being shouted over one another in the attempt to be the first to guess correctly.

Tiny, extended hands wave in the air trying to lay claim to certain guesses before someone else does. I watch it all with mild amusement.

Teachers are needed to contain the many excited voices as they rise with each new guess. Hands clap and whistles are blown to remind us of the rules they have let slide. I would hate to have a teacher with a whistle. That would just make Monday's unbearable.

"Ok. Ok, those are all very good guesses." Mrs. Bell is trying to reclaim the calm of the hallway that was destroyed by her game, before more than just teachers are alerted to the commotion. "I heard someone say brownies. I heard a cake. I even heard pizza which I know was you, Paul."

She's right. It most likely was Paul. The boy loves his pizza. I mean, L-O-V-E-S, his pizza.

"What we have in store for you are some very special, secret recipes, hand made, double chocolate-chip, chocolate cookies!" Her voice grows higher in pitch with each word marking the added excitement to the special treat.

The air around us is almost void with the sudden inhalation of breath the revelation causes. The exhale is a loud celebration of many excited voices. So much chocolate. So many sugar rushes. Totally, unhappy teachers. Yay!

Mrs. Bell and Mrs. Tawny do not even try to help settle the chaos now. They wave like prom queens as they pass through the damage they have caused, smiling at the frustrated teachers as they go. I am pretty certain this is some form of payback with the width of their smiles. The giggles as they turn the corner confirms it for me.

The lunch ladies are proving to be the best style of "busy work" so far this morning. They have successfully removed all thoughts of what lies beyond the double purple doors with the hints of their special treats. Just like Moms that pack special lunches and cook breakfasts into smiling faces, it is all to distract our minds for a few mere moments of comfort. I feel like when Mom figures out the ulterior motive for our actions, but keeps the secret anyway. I keep their secret with a smile as teachers keep it with a glare.

Chapter 6

The loud ruckus does eventually attract the unwanted attention our teachers feared it would. Our principal emerges from the secret chamber to explore the cause for so much chaos. His pressed pants and crisp linen shirt conflicts with the joy crashing against the walls. His look reels in the small celebration in a slow silence of a wave with awareness of him. Our teachers wear an expression of relief and embarrassment with the feelings of inadequacy at needing his help with what is supposed to be their jobs. Whistle Woman just looks mad. I'd hate to be in her class, Monday or not.

"Glad to see so many of you excited for the vaccination this morning," his voice echoes through the hallway without effort, bringing our attention to him fully. It kills the joyful mood completely.

"Since you are already lined up and ready, we will begin to file in. Go ahead and remove any jackets or extra layers of clothing. This will help speed up the process. Once you have received your shot, go ahead and find your teacher and sit in your class rows on the bleachers. We are going to hang out for a while." He gives us the instructions with no more emotion than a fast-talking commercial for prescription medicine. Luckily, there are no reactions to the shot or we may have been here longer as the list was rambled off giving more reasons to not take the medicine than to take it.

Mrs. Lamb is wearing her confused look again. Something that he said has once again set off her alarm bells. Something that, we as kids, have not been picking up on, or maybe just ignoring. The adults in the hall exchange silent glances as each looks to another for hints on the private matter being discussed without words and I wish I had one of those decoder rings offered in the boxes of cereal to help me understand what I am missing. Mine would be purple with pink lights to read the hidden code.

That would so rock. My smile is completely misplaced with the mood around me, but I enjoy the thought anyway.

There is no heavy metal machine set up for us to walk through, like Charlotte said. There are no people dressed in yellow plastic suits with strange hats, like Richard said. There are no men in long white lab coats with clipboards taking notes of our behavior, like Scott said. It is just the school nurse, Miss Lacey, and a plastic chair.

I guess it really is just a shot after all. I shrug with the thought, feeling a morsel braver. A morsel so small, that not even an ant would rejoice in its discovery, but braver just the same.

There is an almost audible exhale with each child that passes through the pastel painted gym doors. The painted mascot on the floor of the gym awaits to welcome us with its smile and an over confident cheer. It is obvious with the shy looks that we are all starting to feel a little silly for so much panic and drama over this.

Our giant train is segmenting as we pass sectioned bleachers. Just as with so many other aspects of school, we are well trained as to where each grade belongs on the many slanted rows of metal benches. Today is no different. We follow without any thought process to our area and climb the metal risers. Our shoes vibrate the walls with the metal echoes of our steps. Even with our newly found courage, we still glance over our shoulders to gain a better perspective of Miss Lacey's actions with each step we climb.

She sits among many plastic cases that appear to be filled with just as many small plastic bags. Her hands tremble some with each motion of preparing for the first class. She is having a hard time meeting the eyes of the Principal as they hold a whispered conversation. It is almost charming to know she is just as anxious about giving the shot as we are about having to receive it.

I've always liked Miss Lacey. She is very giving with her smiles, lollipops, and the bright colored Band Aids that are now stacked and separated in rows of matching colors. Her dark curls gleam with the overhead lights reflecting in their spiraled perfection. Her face that normally fills the room with cheer is dark and dismal with nervous energy. Her shoulders seem to sag today with a heavy weight, robbing her of the glow that normally seems to always follow her, and I am not the only one that notices such a drastic change in our school nurse.

Heads pivot from the metal risers we are climbing, one class at a time, and back to her, watching her motions and trying to gauge the reasons for her new behavior. Courage evaporates like water from a boiling pot. It floats away like the hot steam, fogging the room with our recurring doubts and dark thoughts. It is obvious she feels the many eyes boring into her with how she adjusts her body and squirms in the hard plastic chair.

It is a pastel color, just as everything else is themed in the building. So much thought process was put into forcing cheer into every corner possible. Today, it just seems rude and mocks the true feelings of its inhabitants.

We are selected by grade level as to which classes earn the privilege of going first. Days like this are when being in kindergarten is not as much fun as people had let on. Our cuteness can only save us from so much. Adding the double whammy of Mrs. Lamb having sat on the very bottom of the many tilted benches, forcing our class to line up first, is just depressing. Being the second child in line, that is just unfair.

Why, oh why, didn't I take the back of the line when I had the chance? I ask myself.

Our steps are the smallest they might have ever been in our short lives as we march to the waiting principal. He stands with folded arms and no welcoming posture at all. His eyes bounce over each child and I know he is taking count of how many are lined up before him for whatever reason. His lips are pressed together so tightly that they are losing coloring from the pressure. His cold, business-like demeanor is an extreme opposite of the smiling mascot's face he stands on that welcomed us into the room. He has never been the spokesperson of hugs and comfort, but now, he even steals the joy from nightmares.

There are no more words. No more speeches. No warnings of what is to come. There is just his sharp voice asking our names and marking it from the many crisp white pages on his clipboard. We are to stand beside him as the child before us sits in a chair beside Miss Lacey to receive their vaccine until his pen points us forward. At least, that was the plan in his head. Teddy has a different plan in his head.

"Name?" His eyes do not even glance at Teddy, but prepare to play hunt the name on the sheets. The game never starts though.

"Name?" he calls again. This time his eyes do look over the clipboard, but they are still waiting to play. "Son, what is your name?"

Teddy's voice and legs are locked as he watches the shot being pulled from its plastic prison. The smell of the awaiting alcohol wipe already perfumes the air with a stomach-turning scent. The class clown is now the class leader and he is not finding any of it funny.

Fearing the reaction of our principal's, "no nonsense" attitude, Mrs. Lamb rushes to the front of the line. Her shoes click against the gym floor in her haste to save Teddy from the cold words that may fall upon his already frayed nerves at any moment. She whispers soft words into his ear from a kneeling position that stir minor reactions from him, but he is still not moving forward or offering his name.

His fingers drum against his pants leg as he debates her words. There is no way out of what is ahead of him, but his face shows he is thinking of his options of what to do anyway. His wide eyes show he is in no hurry to believe whatever is being whispered into his ear and the principal's tapping toe shows that he has no patience for the delay. With an adjustment to the clipboard and his posture, I know that Teddy has run out of time. That is when I hear something I never thought I would. Ever.

"Margaret Erikson," I hear my voice betray me. "My name is Margaret Erikson."

I never really offered to go first, but with a brisk swipe of a pen, I am pointed forward. With a gentle reassuring squeeze of my shoulders, I am motioned forward. With a drop of my stomach, I walk forward. I don't think my brain really thought this whole plan out at all.

Teddy owes me his cookies. For real. Is the pout-filled thought that fills my head.

We are always told to "not look". Don't look at the wreck outside the car window. Don't look at the TV when the music gets scary. Don't look under the bed at night. Don't look in the closet after the lights are turned off. Basically, don't look at the monsters. Now the monster is a capped, pointed metal cylinder and I can't stop looking at it.

"It helps if you don't look." Miss Lacey's voice hovers over my panic, repeating the very words I was just mentally debating.

"That's what they say," I reply, backing up her words with my small voice. But, I'm still looking anyway.

"That was a very brave and kind thing you did for Teddy, Margaret." She is roughly rubbing a spot on my arm with the cold, wet wipe. It smells like dread.

"I'm not feeling so brave now." My white-knuckle grasp on my jean jacket proves the truth of my words.

"It will be over before you know it." She winks at me but I don't feel the smile. "Look at your shoes, Margaret, and tell me your favorite color three times."

"Blue." I feel the pinch of the skin to make a steady place for the needle.

"Blue." The sharp tip presses into my skin making my toes curl with the sudden pain.

"Blue." My arm burns like wildfire and I can't hold back the tears that invade my eyes.

"All done," she whispers it, rubbing the spot of the torment. The pain trickles through my arm, making me clench a tight fist as if it can prevent the fire from spreading. She places a blue band aid on my arm, but it brings me no joy as I thought it would. In fact, I am too scared to look up and allow my tears to make me a point of ridicule.

"Teddy is lucky to have such a good friend, Margaret. You were very brave." Miss Lacey rubs my back with more of a forward motion than a comforting gesture. It is the nicest way I have ever been told to move before.

….both cookies. I tell myself as I stand.

I glance backwards, over my shoulder to see if Teddy is finally moving into the seat I just left now that the tension has been broken by my going first. We lock eyes as Miss Lacey begins to repeat the same process with him that I just endured. Our eyes stay with one another until my neck hurts from holding such an extreme position while walking away. I am glad to glance away before the needle is placed into his tender flesh. A girl is only so brave for so long. At least this girl anyway.

Chapter 7

I was the first to sit in the plastic chair of pastel pain and I am the first to sit back on the cold metal bleachers of boredom. That is what they become as we sit and watch each class lined along the center of the gym. It is what they embody as we watch each child call out their name and walk forward, repeating the same process over and over again and our irrational anger grows rapidly. It bubbled inside me almost as soon as I sat down. Now, with most of my class behind me, toes tap in solidarity of an emotion we can't explain the cause of, but something just doesn't feel, "right."

Some names we remark over whose older brother or sister that is. Some names we remark over their clothing choices as our anger mounts. Some names there are no remarks for at all with no knowledge or memory of them. Mostly, each name is just another brisk swipe of a pen on a hidden tally secured to a clipboard. Each mark, one more student down and the tapping grows louder as another joins in.

I don't know exactly when it started or when the pain from my arm reached my head with lightning bright stabs dulling the noises around me. It is so intense that my eyes reactively close with each puncture of the pain. I almost swoon from the sudden heat that rips through my body. My mouth grows dry with it as if the heat has evaporated all water from my body with the burning fire. I am not the only one showing signs of distress. Reactions creep up the rows behind me as if on a timer, colliding into each child with a punch.

Teddy sits beside me shaking his head slowly back and forth in his misery. His breathing is hastened with his pain. He pants, unable to slow his breathing, and I watch him fall to the ground. Mrs. Lamb seems miles away from us. The gym's floor appears to stretch to impossible lengths, pulling her further away from us than it should be possible. I blink, trying to correct my vision, but the corners of the room start to grow black. So, I do the only thing I can think of to signal to our teacher that we need her. I scream.

I scream so loudly, that I stand with the force from it. I stand against the pain that seems to be shredding my brain and against the fire that is roasting inside me. I stand, watching Teddy bounce on the floor beside me with his body's jerking movements. I stand watching my friends fall like a deck of cards, floating slowly in the air one-by-one before they crumple to the floor. I stood to scream for help for those that are around me, but now I am screaming from the terror that is surrounding me.

Taking an unsteady step backwards, away from what is happening on the bleachers, my ankle twists, unable to support me with my body's growing unease. The pain is sharp and almost refreshing as it blocks the pain in my head for a short span of a second. When the second is over, the pain rushes back, stronger than before and I collapse from it. I fall to the cool floor of the gym and stare out at what is happening around me, unable to move anymore.

Like a crowd rolling reverse game of The Wave, bleachers empty from sitting children to be filled with crumpled children. Small bodies jerk in various speeds, banging against the metal of the bleachers or the hard floor of the gym. Skin is splitting and wounds are forming from such a rapid, repeated abuse upon fragile bodies. Red flows down the metal risers like a shiny slinky, pooling at the bottom of the steps in thick puddles.

One puddle forms around me and I want to scream my terror at watching it grow as it encircles me, but I cannot. My vision bounces with my own motions, splashing the thick red blood into a film on my body. It applies a jerking effect to the running teachers through a red haze of my vision as if they are sharing in our suffering, but they aren't.

The gym is now divided into two sections. One section is full with the screams of teachers unable to move to help their students with their own fears, riding them to immobility and the small amount of remaining students that did not receive their vaccine. Those students are being shoved behind adult bodies to protect them from seeing what is happening across the room. They are saved from watching the other section of the gym filling with their friends and siblings beating their bodies to a ruin with jerking convulsions and skull smashing seizures. They scream for them nonetheless.

There are too many breaking bodies. There are not enough teachers to help us. They have no knowledge of what to do to stop any of it, or what is causing it, even if there were. My body feels bruised from the repeated collisions against the hard floor. The heat is cooking me, I know it is. It is too hot to do anything less. Sharp, invisible fingers are tearing my head apart with razor-tipped, pointed nails. I almost hope it will break open from the heat and pain so that it can all escape to the floor to swirl with the blood that coats it. Through all of this, I have no control over my body. I can't scream with the pain. I can't blink away the tears that fill my eyes. I am being forced to stare out blankly at so many eyes that are staring right back at me.

Like the wave that started it, the same motion ends it. The metallic sound slowly fades away as children grow still. Some of the blank stares retreat behind closed eyelids. Some stay open as the color dims from bright shades to dull, glass reflections with life leaving them.

The screams retreat in pitches also with the slowing of time as breaths are held in confusion and fear. The only sounds now filling the room are the thick dripping of the red rivers that flow from the shining metal steps into growing pools of darker coloring. A pool in which I now lie, coating one side of my body with a warm gel feeling.

The last sensation I feel before the room fades from my vision is a sudden explosion of pain in my head. Instead of the white-hot lights that pain sometimes causes, it strips my world of all color. The room becomes shades of gray all around me. The grays become darker and darker as the heat over takes me until there is nothing but blackness surrounding me. I know that my eyes are still open with the raw feeling of needing to blink, but I can see nothing now.

The last sound I hear is Miss Lacey calling my name. She sounds so far away and so sad as she rushes to me, her brave little girl. As I fade into the darkness, I am happy to escape the pain. I am defeated with it.

The pain dissipates as achingly slowly as it built inside me. A part of me whispers that I am dying now, but I don't feel any sadness with that knowledge. I am only saddened that I never got my good-bye hug. I never was able to say good-bye. I was forgotten.

Chapter 8

Awareness comes to me slowly. Inch by inch, my body returns to me with a dull sensation. The hot, scalding fire is gone. The pain is now just an ache that fills a dark void in me. There is commotion all around me that creeps into my mind with a memory. It is a fleeting feeling of something that I feel I should know. I should know, but it flickers and fades before I can fully grasp what it is that I should be remembering. I lose interest in it just as easily as it slipped away.

"Margaret?" I know her voice. It lures me into a higher level of awareness and out of the dark blackness that surrounds me.

"Margaret, can you hear me? Open your eyes." I feel my eyes blink, but it is still only blackness before me. It clears like a cloud of smoke retreating from the wind allowing me to see into the room. The woman is silhouetted at first in a sharp shaded contrast against the lights overhead. I can't see her yet, but I can smell her.

She smells like sweet confectioner's candy floating around me. Like the thick cookies cooling on a counter of a bakery. My mouth grows wet with the scent of her. My body craves things that I don't understand. I don't understand the images that are flashing through my mind's eye. I don't understand the things my body wants me to do to this woman, whose voice I know that I should somehow remember. I have a moment of shame over my weakness. I want to do it all the same though.

My vision clears more, leaving the room in shades of muted colors. Nothing is brighter, or darker, than the basic need for it to be. Light is subdued yet penetrates the dark shadows and allows me to see deeper into them as if I am peering through the tinted lens of sunglasses. My vision is crisp, but muted. Not that it really matters. What I want is right in front of me and I can see her just fine.

She is leaning over me with a flashlight, trying to force its bright beam into one eye and then the other, but I do not blink from it. I can smell her shampoo lingering in the dark curls that cover us like a curtain. Her mouth is moving, speaking to me, but I don't hear the words. Her words are not important. Only the tender flesh of her neck that pulses like a welcoming neon sign holds my focus now. My tongue dances behind my lips with a hunger that I can't explain and a part of me panics with it.

Words are being shouted across the room. Words that hold tones of hope from many female voices as eyes open again. The words that bring a smile to the face floating above me now that my eyes are open. It is the sudden scream that strips that smile just as fast as the words pulled it to her face. We are all awake.

A male voice fills the air with his melody of misery. Joy dances inside me upon hearing it. Horror dances with the woman before me. The sound is as sweet as she smells and when she turns her head to see the cause, I show her the reason behind the screams.

My body instinctively knows just what to do, even if I do not. My hands weave into her thick hair, pulling her neck to my mouth with a strength that I have never used before. I lean up into her with a maddening desire which thrills me and scares me with the same weight of emotion. Her screams pull a response from my body that I shouldn't hold inside me, but I do. It pulls a response that tears out of me as I tear into the sweet meat of her neck like a beast that has been caged and waiting.

Her blood tastes like the thick syrup of honey on my tongue and I am disappointed with every bright red drop that escapes from my mouth. Her flesh is chewy and moist, like a cake surrounding a decadent filling, and I simply can't get enough of her. All panic slides away from me with each mouthful of this woman that slides down my throat.

Even as my mind soothes with my actions, a tiny voice mentally whispers that this is not right. I am not sure what is not right about it, but some small part of me is unsettled by what I am doing. Each bite brings the pain down. It fills the void that was aching inside me. Contentment settles over me like a warm blanket. A blanket that is as red and warm as the blood that fills my throat. The heavy weight of her now still form lulls me into a daze of joy that I want to stay in the thick of forever.

I know there are still screams that surround me. Screams that perk my senses like the music of an ice cream truck in the hot summer's heat. They fill the air with many flavors.

The high pitched screams of terror captivate my attention like exotic spices. The twisting of flavors with the screams of agony are like a perfect combination of sweet and sour. Then for a soothing aftertaste, there are the ones of pleading and defeat. Their taste is subtle and rich like a thick after dinner dessert. Each is tempting in their own way and I, with my new hunger and desires, am lured away from the meal in my mouth now that the rich blood flows slower. It grows thicker against my tongue, losing some of its ripe appeal.

The weight is heavy, but I am able to roll her off of me. The screams reach me in a surround sound of style with the division of the room making them bounce with an echo. There are those, like me, overtaken by a set of new desires that we do not understand, but simply obey. We are blocking out the nagging whispers of uncertainty of our actions fueled by the need to obtain the joyful bliss when the pain stops. The pain that can only be stopped by the moist flesh and syrup of thick fluids that are more refreshing than anything I have ever swallowed before.

Standing before me, we are all testing our new bodies now that the pain has dulled some. My fingers are a duo of jerking and yet gliding motions as I command them to move. My head feels heavy and rests at a slightly lowered angle for ease of position. My eyes are also better from this vantage point. I can see into the deeper shadows and once vivid shades now diminish their hues allowing for better tracking of movements. All around me, those that I know were once more than just replicas of my new self, stand immobilized as hunters, narrowing in on the source of the screams.

Eyes watch as we each pick our new target with self-assured results. They run in various formations trying to flee the room, but in their panic, they have trampled and blocked their own escapes. Terror is blocking their logic and that same terror excites me.

There is no signal that I am aware of given to motion us forward. We just all do. At once, like a pack of animals, we move towards the new meals, stepping over the cold bodies from which we have already fed.

We form into groups built around each other's similarities with the same silent communication displayed before. Each group becomes a strategy of its own to take down the larger prey that we desire. When one of our own falls, with the same sudden force, we freeze, working our minds to find the answer.

She lays fallen and broken, the one that was the nearest of us to the prey. The shade of her hair and the outfit she wears triggers faded memories for me. The brightly colored fabric applied to her upper arm whispers of a lost conversation of sounds that were once words. Words that once we exchanged. A single sound beats against the walls of my mind and I know it belongs to her in some way.

April, it screams, rolling around inside of me.

She was identified once as April, but no longer. We no longer have a need to be identified to one another by these sounds. We flock to one another instinctively.

We find those matching to that of ourselves for protection. When hunting, as we are now, those same groups split to meld into a variety of strengths to better achieve our goal. The goal of stopping the pain.

We stare at her, confused by her sudden loss and the unknown causes, when another falls in the same style. Our minds track the sound that was heard before the last fall. Like truth seeking seers, we find the object that the prey is pointing at us with shaking hands and false brave words. We stare, transfixed by the knowledge our minds report to us.

His pitch does not match the stance his body holds. His hands shake with his fears. It invites us to him. Our anger over his actions and his visible weakness targets his death as the first of many.

We move again, the same sea of us, forward now that we know who is the real threat. Never taking our eyes away from him, our sea parts, forcing him to narrow his attention. His attention may shrink, but his fear grows like ripe fruit on a limb of a sun-drunk tree. It is fragrant and fills us with curiosity of its taste.

His fear grows and festers like a wound left untreated with the panic that adds a new scent to the air. The first group reaches him, dislodging the arm that was holding the object that took two from us. The screams renew with such a volume that all self-restraint is lost. It is stripped from us with such force that not even the nagging whispers we once held can echo over the need. This need that we can no longer fight, but are slaves to and we obey.

With one mind. With one purpose. With one thought. We obey. They fall before us, under us, all around us with our attacks, like fragile toys to a toddler. Sweet syrup sprays against walls. It arches, forming fine modern art before streaking its way back to the ground. It paints the floor from our preys' deaths with each heart that slows under our hungry mouths and brutal hands. We claim this room with our new signatures and when the screaming finally stops, the bliss begins. Mindless, peaceful bliss.

Chapter 9

With the pain now a dull throb, I follow those that a part of me remembers around the room. Sounds flash like lightning when a part of me that I no longer enable recognizes faces or patterns worn around me. The same flash of recognition sparks on faces as I walk by. There is no emotion tied to the responses. Just the fact that they are there. I hold no remorse for the one who belongs to the sound of April, who lies as still as the discarded prey now on the painted floor. I hold no joy for the boy that walks beside me even if his blue cloth streak on his arm spurs the whispers again. We walk together not out of a bond of emotions, but for protection with exploration.

A part of us knows, even with the sheer number of us now roaming, that we are the enemy. We are the enemy to those that screamed at the sight of us, providing us with clues that we have stored for future use and for our survival. There is something that sets us apart from those that look like us, but fear us. A something that causes them to fight us with more than just the need for their own survival. They are more than just food for us and we are more than just death for them.

We explore, as a group, the new pluses and minuses of our bodies. For some of us, movements are slower. Legs slide, more than glide, across the floor with the new language our brains speak. Some move like shadows, creeping with ease and high anxieties. Eyes either stare ahead or continue to scan for movements around them. There seems to be a defining difference in us. As if some have lost a "spark" or never contained it to begin with and now it is only more obvious.

Those without, "the spark" are quickly left behind in their own groups. They are ignored by those of us who see them as a "weak link," making them a future threat. A few of the most obvious "weak links" are brutally taken down by the shadows.

There is no tasting of their flesh or exploitation of their deaths. They are ended abruptly and suddenly without so much as a pause of a thought to the action. I feel no remorse for them either.

My body responds well to my thoughts. My fingers tear when I need them to, reaching the depths of the hot, hidden meat encased in the fragile bones of my prey. My teeth clamp and shred flesh and muscles alike, like candy flavored wrappings. The only difference between those that walk with me in this new style of exploration and myself is the foot that hinders me.

It falters with my full weight, forcing me to move with more effort when stalking. There is a whisper from the dark corner of my mind with a reason for it, but it never fully reaches me. I don't really need it to. There is no pain connected to the failing body part and I have adapted with the loss of limb. I have learned how to deal with the limitations placed on that side of my body and it is no more of a detour to death than a moment of time is to a life.

With our hungers now fed, most of us have stopped our motions and explorations. We rest, letting our minds shut down in some basic understanding of how to store the fuel to power our bodies that are being converted. My mind doesn't so much as wander but becomes mute.

I am still aware of those around me. I am just not invested in their activities anymore. There is no need for me to fill the time. I simply wait for whatever may be next like a bird in a cage with a blanket thrown over it to sleep.

Chapter 10

How long I have stood here in my muted existence, I don't know. I hold no value in time or have anything to associate with its passing. All that marks the span of time now is the moments between bliss and pain and the pain is building.

It snakes into my awareness, stirring my mind into a higher level of "awake". The blanket is being drawn away slowly like a parting curtain on a stage show. The actors are coming into focus and they are feeling the same stirrings as me. The hunger is back and it brings suffering.

The pain is a sharp twisting of pangs like contorting muscle cramps. The cramps clench and spread through my body before releasing me from their grasps, only to clamp down again. Each clamp tightens deeper into me. With each retreat of the clenching that rolls over me, pain and anger expand in the space left.

A nagging need to destroy something filters through every thought. The only way to ease this torment is to feed. I have to fill my mouth and throat with the death of something. Something that is warm and flowing hotly down my throat. I must take life into me to fuel my own. It is not a matter of enjoyment of the act just the satisfaction of the result.

My eyes scan the room with my body still locked tight from movement. I don't want to startle any prey that may be near me with a sudden movement. It is better to stay frozen, moving only my eyes until I find what my body is desiring. This makes sense to some part of me that I have never known. This scares the part of me that is still trying to call out in despair over what I am learning.

A few have fallen on the broken shells that still hold warmth in their depths. The blood is thick and dark. I know this means there is not enough warmth to entice me to join them. Their torment is greater than mine. I have not sunk to their depths of desperation yet, reducing me to their needs. I haven't yet, but with each mounting cramp, I may still.

With nothing to spook by my presence, my mind releases my body from its cage. Like an ocean wave, we begin to walk again with some hope of finding something to hunt. We are less animated now with less fuel for our bodies.

The weaker ones drag along red walls coated like a candy apple, smearing the sweet icing with their bodies. The "shadows" are still, watching us with eyes that catalog every one of our movements. Even to me, their actions send a warning of apprehension for reasons I can't label. It is enough for me to navigate my path further from them and their motives of survival of the fittest.

A whimpering of a sound comes to me as I pass one huddled over a carcass. She is pulling thick meat from deep inside the cage of bones that causes a wet sloshing sound. There is something about the shading of the shirt she wears that pulls my eyes and a soft caress of a whisper.

Charlotte I hear from a hidden collection of knowledge.

Charlotte and Schinder it displays for me in meaningless sounds.

Charlotte feeds with desperation and almost mewing sounds. Her needs are overriding what our minds understand. There is no life to feed from left to this cold casing. The blood is already a thick black shading, not the red shade of warmth that fresh prey holds. The darker the blood, the colder the meat. The blood must be red. It just has to be.

My body locks with a clue of something new being near. Something that I was not aware of just moments ago has pulled us all into a hunting stance. Our eyes scan the area while our bodies remain still, afraid of missing a chance to feed. It is a soft sound. A gentle sound that opens up a memory for me. It is not so much a memory as a clue to guide my hunt. It is a hint helping me locate my prey. A simple picture of something that is linked to the sound and I know where to find it.

In unison, our eyes swing to the metal doors of the room. Doors that we have forgotten about without the need to open them. Until now that is. Now, standing there in the small gap of space is prey. Prey that stares back at us with the same surprise we have. It is shocking to find so many of us watching it and we are shocked by the discovery of an exit. An exit that may lead us to more food and greater bliss. It is a way out of this prison and into the world beyond.

Once again, we are a sea of destruction. The "shadows" are the first to move like foam of a wave that hits the beach first. We are the crest that follows, with great force, directly behind. Behind us, are the weaker ones, but all together we form an army of hunger and dark desires that propels us forward into the madness that now overtakes us.

There are two that rush from us. One younger, of our ages, sun spun blonde hair and delicate ivory skin that turns my mouth into a wet cavern of desires. The other is the very meaning of her opposite. She is older and of dark hair and fills my senses with an imagined taste of smoky spices. The second one is shouting sounds of fear that spur my hunger into a dark void of a frenzy but the blonde has stopped moving a few feet from behind the door.

The space left by the open doors is small and confined. It is a narrow mouth of escape until its imaginary jaws are worked open from the sheer force of our numbers. I hear our bodies expressing our excitement with attempts of vocal exclamations but it is disjointed and muddled. It is nothing as eloquent as the sounds that my mind associates with the ones I hold recognition for, nor is it as punctuating as the sounds coming from ahead of us. It is an almost mockery of an attempt to communicate, but it frees the pent up aggression just the same. The sounds also seem to stir a deep level of panic in our prey. Panic that will pump through the heated blood, giving the meat an added flavor for us to enjoy. All we must do is reach the meat.

The blonde is no longer responding to the sounds from the older brunette. She is planted to the spot in the hallway that is losing the distance between us. Her head is turned away from her impending doom, yet it does not lessen our hunger for her. She might not be fueling my excitement, but she will be fuel nonetheless.

Another memory comes to mind, but the hunger pushes it away before I can take real notice. The boy that now comes into view, his spark I can't extinguish. It is more than just sounds that trigger this spark. I have knowledge of him. Almost moments of images that try to piece themselves together in my mind.

Conroy. He is Conroy, a sound I know. A sound that links the rest of them together.

Conroy. Ashley. Helena. These are the three before me now. Three that belong to another time and another life.

It stirs my curiosity at seeing him before me now and yet back then at the same time in my mind. Unfortunately, the curiosity does not match the level of interest I hold to reach the bliss again. The bliss that is the only way for me to remove the feelings of my pain and fulfill the cravings that propel my actions. Curiosity that is easily forgotten as he sinks back to only being food. He, like the other two, is only a way to stop the torment.

The first wave has reached the first target. The screams that fill the air around me are not hers, but those of the other. The brunette, Helena, screams with a raw emotion as we overtake our meal.

We tear into her so fast with our greed that there is no time for any screams from Ashley beneath our flesh-raping hands and the tearing of tiny, pointed teeth. It is a total destruction to her body with so many of us competing to gather even the smallest of handfuls. The fragile casing is torn asunder, coating the walls with our greed.

Soon, just as every time before, our new toy breaks under our enjoyment and the red turns black, the meat turns cold, and my interest is no longer on being a competitor for one, but the chance to dine on a whole. A whole that is now running away.

Chapter 11

I am no longer curious about the knowledge of past interactions with the boy or his sisters. I don't care how I hold such images of him. All I want to know right now is how his flesh feels under my fingers when I pull it apart. I want to know the heat of the temperature his heart beats and the rhythm of how it pumps. My curiosity is now over his soft candy center and his sweet liquid filling.

Which flavor will his fear give it?

Will it be a thrilling amber spice with an exotic tingle? Will it pour hotter and faster from him with the increased beating of his heart? Or, will it hold hints of garlic and spices from the earth, catering to a more basic nature? All I have to do is find him to find all of these answers and perhaps even more.

I separate from the sea like a lone ripple, casting myself outwards of the inner circle. My mind has already crawled back inside a crate, locking the pain away, so that I may focus on the hunt. A "shadow's" eyes watch me while his hands work independent from his attention. They seem to automatically know where to reach, bringing cupped handfuls to his mouth without any need for coaching from his senses. I adjust my path so that I am not in the reach of those all knowing hands. Only once his eyes have reached the extent of their range does my mind ease down and truly focus on finding my answers. The answers a little boy holds buried inside him like a treasured secret.

Their retreat echoes off the plaster walls making the source difficult to locate with so many returns of the vibrations. The brunette's path is easier to follow. As if she has left me a trail of clues, I can smell the smoke that clings to her, giving me a hint of her flavoring. Like a seductress wears perfume to lure her victims to her, this one is wearing the scent to become a victim. My mind projects a path for me to take and I follow it. Life is no longer about the many questions or the over thinking of actions. I just do. If I am well fed, I rest. If something hurts, I feed it. If something moves, I kill it. Any deeper needs than that, I have none.

The pain is building to a blinding pressure of sharp stabbing and tearing. Each cramp feels to be shredding a thick piece of me, as if I should be leaving parts behind me as I travel. My body slows from the agony it causes even as my mind presses me forward. This new part of me knows something that I am not being so lost in this haze of pain. I am about to discover my answers.

"Margaret?" It is a small voice. An almost whisper with fear holding the volume at bay. My body reacts the way it has become trained to do.

I become immobile, only my eyes roll slowly to the source of the sound, keeping my motions from giving away my intentions. My foot even pauses in mid-step, waiting to see if the sound will repeat itself.

"Margaret?" It comes again, a little bolder this time, lured into the safety net of my inactions. I softly reposition myself to pivot in his direction, stalking the sound of him so that I will be ready for any attempt of escape again. My body pulls into itself, hiding the truth of me and the threat of the danger I present. My hair sways even with the effort of looking harmless, adding its own illusion of safety to my performance.

The brunette, once again, ruins our game. I hear her voice hiss a warning to him. It will pull him from me and I will lose my chance. My body clenches with the anger over her actions and the pain of my hunger. I won't lose him again, and if she gets in the way, then she too can feed my suffering.

His head turns away as mine turns, too. It is a perfect moment in time for a hunter and its prey, keeping the prey safe and secure in its little trap of peace. He is only a few wide steps from me. I can smell his soft flesh. It floats to me with a trail of mouth-watering aroma blended together with the smell of him and the smell of his clothing. Hunger combats my mind's calm, rational plan for his murder. It flashes pictures inside my head of how to proceed. It shows me how to obtain my goals and I obey. I have no deeper needs than that.

My fingers tighten and hook into the perfect tearing weapons to shred his flesh. My body becomes motivated and pitches forward, forgetting my unresponsive leg for a brief moment. A moment that motivates her with needs of her own. We are both in a race to reach the boy for different reasons. I want his death. She wants his life. For one to become the winner, the other has to become the loser.

He never saw me. Nor did he feel the mere space of air that my hand missed him, but she did. Her panic is a musky perfume with her smoky undertones. She might not be the seductress she intended, but she seduces my senses all the same. I am so impassioned by her scent, and what it whispers to my tongue, that I do not grow angry when she steals him from me. It only adds to the game now. I originally set out to find him, now my mouth is watering for her.

I do not run after them as I watch her run from me. I smile to the boy that now stares at me over her shoulder, letting him know that I am coming. His wide eyes know that I am coming.

Run if you like, but I am coming.

She slips rounding the first corner and I know she will not get far.

Run. Run as fast as you can. Tire yourself out. Find a spot to hide, thinking you are safe from me and from your death. My body does not need to rest or recover. I will not grow tired. I will find you. So run, run until your heart gives out, because I am coming.

Chapter 12

It didn't take long for the others to catch up to me. The "shadows" crept into the space with silent movements and watching eyes. Their eyes being the only acknowledgment of me with their slow stare and a general assessment of my actions. They are aware that while they hung back for one, I was hunting two. With what part of me accepts as respect, they do not pass my steady pace as they easily could. Instead, we keep the pace of the group with eye contact and silent communication as we continue in our hunt.

The dark part of me that enjoys the sensation of fear in my victims, knows that the same sensation could be used against me if I allow those now crowded around me to sense it. A blank resolve to stay calm settles over me because no one understands the hunt better than the hunters.

Her scent is easy to follow. It is as if it tugs on me to come forward with ghostly fingers, leading me straight to her death. Half of me is elated with how easy this is proving to be. Another half of myself is disappointed in the simple foundation of the game. For it to end in such an uneventful trend, yet again, leaves me feeling robbed of a victory that I do not understand.

Her scent is hiding behind a metal barrier that blocks our path. An image of what this is flashes in my mind. It's showing me the function and purpose of it, helping me to comprehend how to defeat her escape. The "shadows" twitch as they stare at it. Their minds formulating a path through it faster than mine.

It gives easily under the force of their shove, swaying into the room before swaying back to us. A harder shove results in the barrier swinging wider before returning. We smile, grasping the concept and with one more solid shove, the barrier's secret is removed.

We pour into the room with eager mouths and deadly thoughts. Her scent wraps around me like the music of a far away ice cream truck, exciting me with her tune, but she only leaves me hungry for more because just like the truck of frozen treats, she is not here. The room is empty, void of her and the melody of comfort.

Her scent is everywhere. I should be walking around her as if she is the flowers of a blooming garden, filling the air with their fragrance. I can also smell the boy. He is a soft under current of gentle hints and fragile promises. He is here too, somewhere.

The room is wide and easy to see in every angle. There are no places to hide, keeping them from us. The objects are too tall, or too thin, to shield them from us. No corners to crouch around, peering bravely at us from a hidden shadow of security. Nope, this room is bare and void of our prey. There is just their scent lingering in the air to taunt us and mock our hunger.

I know this room. I have spent many afternoons huddled around the tall objects placed throughout. Faded sounds of laughter and the loud clattering of plastic trays play through my mind like an old black and white movie. The colors are not the only aspect missing with the facts hidden from me. I know the sound attached to the room though.

Cafeteria. The sound tells me nothing more than of syllables and lost memories.

Confusion fades before swelling to anger and then fades back to emptiness with no other action left to me. Remotely, I follow those that resemble my own features in size and shape. I block my thoughts, trying to escape the aching and burning torment that feels to be mutilating my body from within. We shuffle in clumps and lines, keeping to our own, with the hopes of keeping our minds busy on any action that will help distract from the pain. A pain that only seems to crest with each wave of her scent that reaches me before the current pulls me back into its hateful grasp.

With nothing more to do now than to walk and endure, pictures randomly insert themselves into my vision. The random pictures of smiles and faces that stir a moment of a trickle of remembrance for a time I have forgotten inside me. Moments of emotions associated with such faces whisper to me like an old friend that I should know. Some of the pictures match up, in a small way, to those around me. The whispers tell me that I should I know them. I should know them all, but I don't, not really.

There are the sparks and flashes again of attempts for a feeling when I notice one or another, but nothing solid. It is the same again for the others. Our eyes meet, and for a brief pause, there is a second of connection, but in general, it fades and we are left as we are now. We are aware of each other, but unaware of who or what we are. We are nothing more now than hunters. We are monsters that cause screams at our sight. We don't seek the smiles the pictures flash in my mind's eyes. We don't embrace each other with grins and joyful laughter. We walk, or stand, together for protection, not for any building of emotional interactions. We hunt. We eat. We wait. We repeat.

Chapter 13

Three tones and the room becomes a garden of small statues instantly. Feet are raised, heads are cocked, bodies balance with the constant shift of required weight all while we try to assess what has happened. But there is something else we are straining to grasp, too. There was another sound that rang out through the room. A sound our minds pique with the yearning our bodies crave. Prey.

It was a high-pitched scream of stark fear and the boy with the blue cloth stuck to his arm had found the source first. There is another set of barriers once again blocking our exploration. Barriers that we had not noticed until now that are holding the sound of our target behind them. The riddle of the last barrier is still fresh in our minds.

The boy applies the same test to them, watching them sway slightly from his hand. He smiles with the simple mechanism of the blockage and pushes harder, catching one with the same hand. With a pause, he waits for us to gather behind him. His body is tense with the anticipation of what may lie on the other side. Like soldiers, we file in behind him waiting for a signal to come. His arm is ready to open the door and we will march, not to defend, but to destroy.

The chime comes again, three loud sharp tones with no pattern other than a basic repeating, and it brings forth the signal we were waiting for. His scream is an invitation. It is the power held by a motivational speaker on a high stage, spurring others into action and we act with it.

The door is shoved open, allowing no hidden space between it and us. It grows stuck on some hidden spring, giving us an edge in our game with its wide, welcoming space held open. There is nothing to segment our formation now with irregular closings that would limit the number of us entering at a time. We are a long line of hunger and shades of desperation.

I know it is her before I am able to enter the room. The scent that has been playing peek-a-boo with me is now heavy in the air. It hangs like a thick fog on a fall morning. I can see through it, but it coats me with each step I take until I am wearing it as if it is mine. But this scent is hers. She has trademarked it and claimed it in my memory and I can't wait to taste it. I want to feel it roll over my tongue before it slides down my throat. My hunger pulses with the pain now that I know she is so close to me.

Our minds retreat into a world of prey and predator. We match their every backwards step with one of a forward. We are keeping the perfect pace with the prey to not trigger a fight or flight feeling from them. Our eyes become mind readers that stay and lock on panicked faces with our calm thoughts that project no need for any rush. We are given clues with the body language of our meal as to how to adjust our hunt. We are told when to speed up, or keep pace. We watch, trying to guess any changes in their behavior. We wait, yearning for the signal that will tell us when the time is right to take them.

It is a tango of death. A dance full of stiff movements with locked arms and blank faces. It is hard to tell who is the leader of this dance. Are we leading them, or are they leading us? With the change in the brunette, it is easy to see the dance is about to come to an end.

Her eyes glance around with too much white exposed by her fears. She is looking for an out that is not to be found. There are no more long hallways to run from us. There is not a barrier to place between us, hiding her from us. There are just makeshift rows of an alleyway that lead us deeper into the new room.

I told you I would find you. I smile with the thought.

There is a shift in the brunette. Her body language hints at a discovery she is trying to shield from us. I am not the only one to figure this out with the air of a mood swing around us. Our calm veneer is wearing thin with the constant pressure to remain docile and the hunger that fights against it.

Fingers flex, fantasizing with the thoughts of their soft flesh under them. Feet shuffle in a haste to reach the blocked space ahead of them, resulting in a faltering of ranks. Placid faces pull back, showing the true monsters that we are. The game is over. The dance is ending. We are no longer hunting. We are ready to kill.

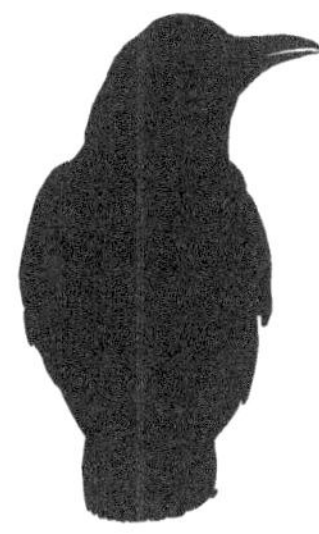

Chapter 14

His screams fill my ears and it thrills me. There are words in his raised voice, but it is the sheer sound of it that matters to me. His fear vibrates the room with his small voice. The voice is weak and yet forceful with the loud shouting of his emotions. It rolls our eagerness inside us with a force from behind a thick dam until it bursts forth, unable for it to be restrained any longer.

She has attempted to block us again with a thick reflective barrier. The boy that has finally stirred our inner nature is secure behind it. Our army crashes against its mirror surface with the full force of our disappointment as we are being cheated again from our need. Disappointment rips through us and out with sounds of desperation for him.

The handle that she used to open it is too high for our outstretched arms. Fingers dislocate, snapping and popping as our mind forces our bodies to find him. Shoulders are brought out of joint with our minds wrought with anger and need, destroying these fragile shells of ours. We feel none of it. Only the cramps that are clutching us with a madness all to its own. We feel only the pain from the hunger that we are unable to satisfy now.

His screams still fill the air even blocked from us like this. It is a mingling of fear and pain from within this metal closet in the kitchen. There are pictures that are spread over the doors of two women which are set in the same backdrop of this room. The whispers come again. I know these smiles that we are destroying with our efforts to figure out this riddle. Moments of time are shown to me from memories I hold in another part of me. A part that is still fighting to hold on as I fight to let it go.

Mrs. Bell. Mrs. Tawny. That part of me is begging me to remember. Almost pleading with me to remember, coaxing me back to another state of mind. My mind, my new mind, doesn't have a need or room for such a life. It would only defeat my new purpose. I can't have that, and the whispers are shut away, placed back in the darkest of corners that I won't explore.

We are so mindless with our focus on him, that we have forgotten his partner. A scent that drove me to a level of madness, I had put out of my mind with the easy target of the one so simple to spark with fear. Fear that triggers the beast inside of me that is needed to do what I need to happen.

Her scream now dances on my conscious, pulling my attention back to the predator. My body shuts down and lets my mind and its hidden beast take over. They work as one, giving my body commands, gliding it into action. The anger I was feeling washes away leaving my face back to a mask of preparation. Pain, and all its torment, is muted so I may focus on her. So that I may destroy her.

My head tilts to gain a better view of her. To watch her as my body glides forward, becoming a barrier myself to the boy that she let slip away. Her scent is not the same. It does not have the sharp musk of panic anymore. It is a blend of softer undertones with her normal smoky flavoring. This unsettles a piece of me and I focus harder on her actions.

My eyes follow her hand. Its random movements against the wall tell me that she is searching for something. She is looking for a way to defend herself and another instance that has this same feeling comes to mind.

Like what they did that stopped April. I can see the one like me falling to the floor while we stood there pondering the cause of the noise. A moment that allowed the prey to remove those from us, reducing our numbers and our protection, just as she is searching to do now.

Anger at the thought of such a weak creature looking to harm me triggers the beast in me. I can already taste her flesh in my mouth with the hate that I have for her now. She thinks she can not only escape, but destroy us. The prey does not become the hunter. Hunters just become better killers.

The "shadows" are the first to sense the change. I can feel them bringing their focus to her without having to look for her. The noise behind me fades as each becomes aware, finally, of the threat. They are the frozen moments of time when our minds switch modes, but I know it will be a short pause. We are too hungry for our minds to let more time than is needed to slip past us.

Her hand grasps what I know will be something used to harm me if I allow her and the noise it makes when she claims it snaps her into the center of their thoughts. I cannot wait for them to catch up to me if I am to stop her. If she is to be prevented from escaping again, if we are to feed, I must face her on my own with hopes that they will join in shortly.

The beast is taking over fully. My face is no longer mine. It now belongs to the beast that stalks inside me. I feel my lips pull back into the glare and rage it knows how to wear. All thought processes are removed with its presence inside me. I am nothing now but the simple needs of one that must feed. Her body is the key to my salvation and survival. There is nothing to debate. There is nothing to rationalize. I must feed. She must die. It is so simple that it is almost freeing.

There is a moment when our eyes lock and I know she is seeing something different than that of what I am. I know that she is comparing me to the one that screams for her behind the door. The one that she sought to save from us, but her tears hint at a failing to do so. It was just a moment. A mere flash of regrets before she gathered herself. Her scent changes with it. She is no longer the prey in her mind. I am.

She screams with her attack upon me. The knife reflects the lights in the room, seeming to glow as she plunges it into my body. There is a flutter of panic with a thought to the damage it should cause me, but there is nothing.

The blade is not cold or burning pain. It is nothing more than air. There is no pain, no obvious answer yielded by its mutilation. Without the pain, my beast never retreats. It rides my surface, seeking any opening to harm her and it finds one.

Her arm is so close to my face that I can almost see her pulse at her wrist beating in the deep blue veins. They are straws that I may sip on, pulling the hot, sweet syrup that I crave into my mouth. I want them.

I turn my head, seeking those straws with my teeth. Teeth that feel like days ago were just sinking into soft flesh, allowing me to reach the bliss. A bliss that I am denied with her continued fighting me. I didn't feel her knock me down, but I am falling away from her just the same. Falling to the ground in a similar state that I started all of this in.

I am not a monster. I am just so hungry! Why won't you help me? My mind pleads with her to understand my need of her, but it is only anger I feel staring up at her.

I stand slower than normal. Something is pouring from me, from the place that she attacked me. With no pain to trigger any of what was once a way to know when I am in danger, I head towards her again, but I won't reach her. I will never satisfy this hunger, but my pain will end just the same.

I'm not a monster. I just want the pain to stop. She may not have saved those she came with, but she saves me. She ends my suffering.

Chapter 15

She cries for me as she takes my life. If this is a life? The beast retreats, knowing it is beaten, leaving me to face these moments alone. With that part of me silent, the whispers take over. The part of me that has fought so hard against being kept in the dark corners of my consciousness now is here to help me understand everything that the beast has kept hidden.

I fall, broken and doomed at her feet. I watch, just as I watched once before in my final moments, my once friends destroyed by something again out of their control. Lives fade with, not the blood we sought after, but with our own flowing together on the floor in a thick puddle of defeat. We were not monsters. We were victims, and we have become victims again.

I remember everything now. I remember the laughter of my friend April, the one we lost first. How ironic it was, her being so afraid of the dead things. She was always so timid and shy with her many fears. She was never a monster. Just the one they killed first.

I remember how afraid Teddy was of the shot that took our freedom and how, in this new form, he took the lead, no longer a scared little boy hiding behind jokes to mask his shyness. He had no say then and he had no control now. He was not a monster. Just a little boy that was afraid of the pain and then only wanted for the pain to stop.

I remember the sound of my mother's voice as she sang to me trying to calm my fears. She sang a song that I took for granted each morning, and now I will never hear again. She told me she was going for her shot this afternoon. I can't warn her to save her. No one will ever hear her sing again. She won't be a monster. Just a mother that is lost to me forever.

My father, with his over scheduled day, will never make it to his afternoon appointments. They will judge him as I did. They will think he has forgotten them the way I thought the same of him. He will, but not because he wants to. He won't have the option to remember them. He is not a monster. Just a man that worked so hard for so long to provide for his family that he wasn't always perfect. But who is?

We will never be rewarded for being so brave this morning like we were told we would. Our reward is our death. It was given to us not with smiles and pretty bows, or even with the warm chocolate cookies we were promised, but with pain and the tears of remorse for having to do it. We will never feel the love of those that care for us again. We were not monsters, but that is how we will be remembered in shared stories and haunting nightmares. We were just children.

My final death is so much easier than the last. There is no pain this time. Just a draining feeling like when the night comes after a long day and all you want to do is sleep, to just escape. One last sigh, and I escape.

Chapter 16

"Margaret…." Miss Lacey is calling to me again. I don't want to answer her. I don't want to face what I have done to her.

"Margaret, can you hear me? Open your eyes." The same words again, and I am so haunted with fear of them.

Why won't it just end?

"Open your eyes, Margaret. We are waiting for you." Her voice pulls me forward out of the blackness once again and they are here. They are all waiting for me.

Surrounded by laughter and smiles, they are waiting for me. Teddy, April, Meghan, are all here running among our friends and even Charlotte with her make-up and bright colors waves to me. Miss Lacey stands beside me, smiling, and I am filled with shame with the taste of her still so fresh in my mind.

A feather-soft kiss she places on my forehead and I know that I am forgiven for my sins. We all are. Those that were killed and those that killed mingle with warm hugs and reassuring smiles. Our clothes no longer wear the stains of our actions. It is as if it was all a bad dream. A dream that we are all waking up from now with each new child that appears and is forgiven by whom they harmed.

The bell rings its three sharp tones, bringing the day back to order and my friends turn, waiting on me to join them.

"What is my brave girl waiting on?" Miss Lacey asks me, with her heart-soaring smile.

"I'm afraid," my voice is tender with my fears and shame.

"What is there to be afraid of?" Her smile continues, earning my trust to confide with her.

"The monsters," I whisper it, knowing the secret shame the words hide.

"There are no more monsters, Margaret. There will never be any more monsters here. Just us. Just your friends. Forever." I smile at her words and the relief it causes deep inside me.

With a skip, I rush to join my friends in our new world. A world where we are surrounded by friendships and laughter. Laughter that will now echo off of pastel teal and purple empty halls that will soon decay with the lack of life another world has now.

Swings will swing as if by a breeze but it will be us. Tiny footsteps will roam the shadows in games of tag and hide and seek and it will be us. Nursery rhymes will be chanted with the clacking of a rope on the cold floor, and it will be us.

Doors will open, laughter will be heard, and it will always be us, safe in a world of our making. Horrors will wait for those that come now, but not for us. We are free. We have escaped. We were never the monsters. We were just children and children we will forever now be.

About the Author

Marie F Crow weaves her stories around the human element of the horror verses the 'monsters' themselves. She believes that the real horror of life does not come from the expected, but from the unexpected responses of the human nature and what depths of trauma a person must survive in certain situations. She began writing The Risen series when feeling that the popular genre was slipping too deep into the realm of pure 'slasher' and forgetting what the horror of zombies can mean for a story.

Now, with her children's series launched, Marie hopes to use her favorite 'monster' as a teaching tool to inspire children to understand that not everything that looks scary, is scary. With Abigail and Her

Pet Zombie series, Marie hopes to further spread her love for all things "that go bump in the night" with small children showing them that it's okay to be different and to embrace those same differences in those around them.

Social Media Links
Facebook: @MarieFCrow.Author
Instagram: @authormariefcrow
Twitter: @MarieFCrow

Additional titles by Marie F Crow:

The Risen Series
Dawning
Margaret
Remnants
Courage
Defiance

The Siren Series
Betrayal of the Crown

The Abigail and her Pet Zombie Series
Abigail and her Pet Zombie
Zoo Day
Spring
Summer
Halloween

About the Publisher

Kingston Publishing offers an affordable way for you to turn your dream into a reality. We offer every service you will ever need to take an idea and publish a story. We are here to help authors make it in the industry. We've been hurt by publishers in the past and we want to provide a positive experience that will keep you coming back to us.

Whether you want a traditional publisher who offers all the amenities a publishing company should or an author who prefers to self-publish, but needs additional help - we are here for you.

Now Accepting Manuscripts!

Please send query letter and manuscript to:

submissions@kingstonpublishing.com

Visit our website at www.kingstonpublishing.com

9 781645 337867